For Marion x ~ A. R.

For Nicole and David x x x ~ H. G.

Copyright © 2012 by Good Books, Intercourse, PA 17534
International Standard Book Number: 978-1-56148-745-5
Library of Congress Catalog Card Number: 2011031770

Text copyright © Alison Ritchie 2012
Illustrations copyright © Hannah George 2012
Original edition published in English by Little Tiger Press,
an imprint of Magi Publications, London, England, 2012
LTP/1500/0287/1011 • Printed in Singapore

Library of Congress Cataloging-in-Publication Data

Ritchie, Alison.
Duck says don't! / Alison Ritchie ; [illustrated by] Hannah George.
p. cm.
Summary: When Goose goes on vacation, Duck finds out that
being in charge and keeping the pond the happiest pond in
the world is much too hard.
ISBN 978-1-56148-745-5 (hardcover : alk. paper)
[1. Bossiness--Fiction. 2. Ducks--Fiction. 3. Geese--Fiction.
4. Ponds--Fiction. 5. Pond animals--Fiction.]
I. George, Hannah, ill. II. Title. III. Title: Duck says do not.
PZ7.R51155Du 2012
[E]--dc23
2011031770

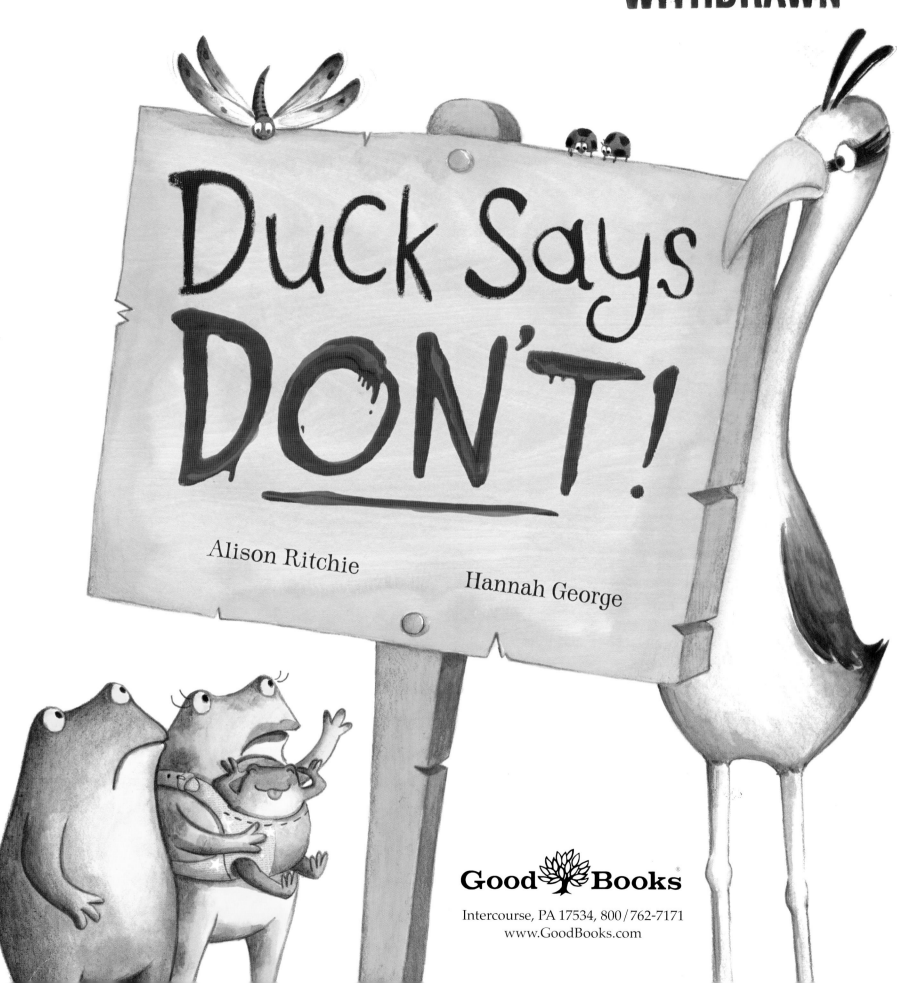

Duck Says DON'T!

Alison Ritchie

Hannah George

Good Books

Intercourse, PA 17534, 800/762-7171
www.GoodBooks.com

Duck lived on Goose's pond.
It was a **beautiful** pond. The water
was clear and sparkly, the sun shone,
and everyone was **happy**.

One day Goose told Duck, "I have a **very** important job for you. I'm going on vacation, and I want **you** to look after the pond while I'm away."

Duck couldn't believe it.

"I am in **charge!**" he thought.

"Goose, I will do my very best," he promised.

The next day Duck was up early watching over his beautiful pond. Suddenly he spotted the dragonflies racing.

"Stop that!" he quacked. "You should **not** be buzzing about all over the pond!"

FINISH LINE

"We're flying, Duck," said the dragonflies.
"That's what we do!"
    "Not here you don't,"
said Duck.

"I told them," he thought.
But just to make sure,
Duck fetched some
wood, and hammered
late into the night…

The next morning there was a sign in the pond.

Later that day, Duck saw Kingfisher fishing.
"Stop that!" he shouted.
"Fishing is not allowed here."

"Then where can I fish?"
asked Kingfisher.
"Somewhere else!" snapped Duck,
and he waddled off with his bottom in the air.

He fetched more wood and got busy
with another sign.

Duck was having a little nap when
the frogs dived into the water.

SPLASH!

"What do you think you're doing?" Duck yelled. "Diving is forbidden!"

"Forbidden?" asked the frogs angrily. "Says who?"
"Says me," snapped Duck. "Duck! I'm in charge of the pond!
So get out right now!"

Soon there were signs **everywhere**!

NO DIVING
Diving is STRICTLY Forbidden
(because Duck says so!)
NO RUN
NO SPLASHING
NO SW

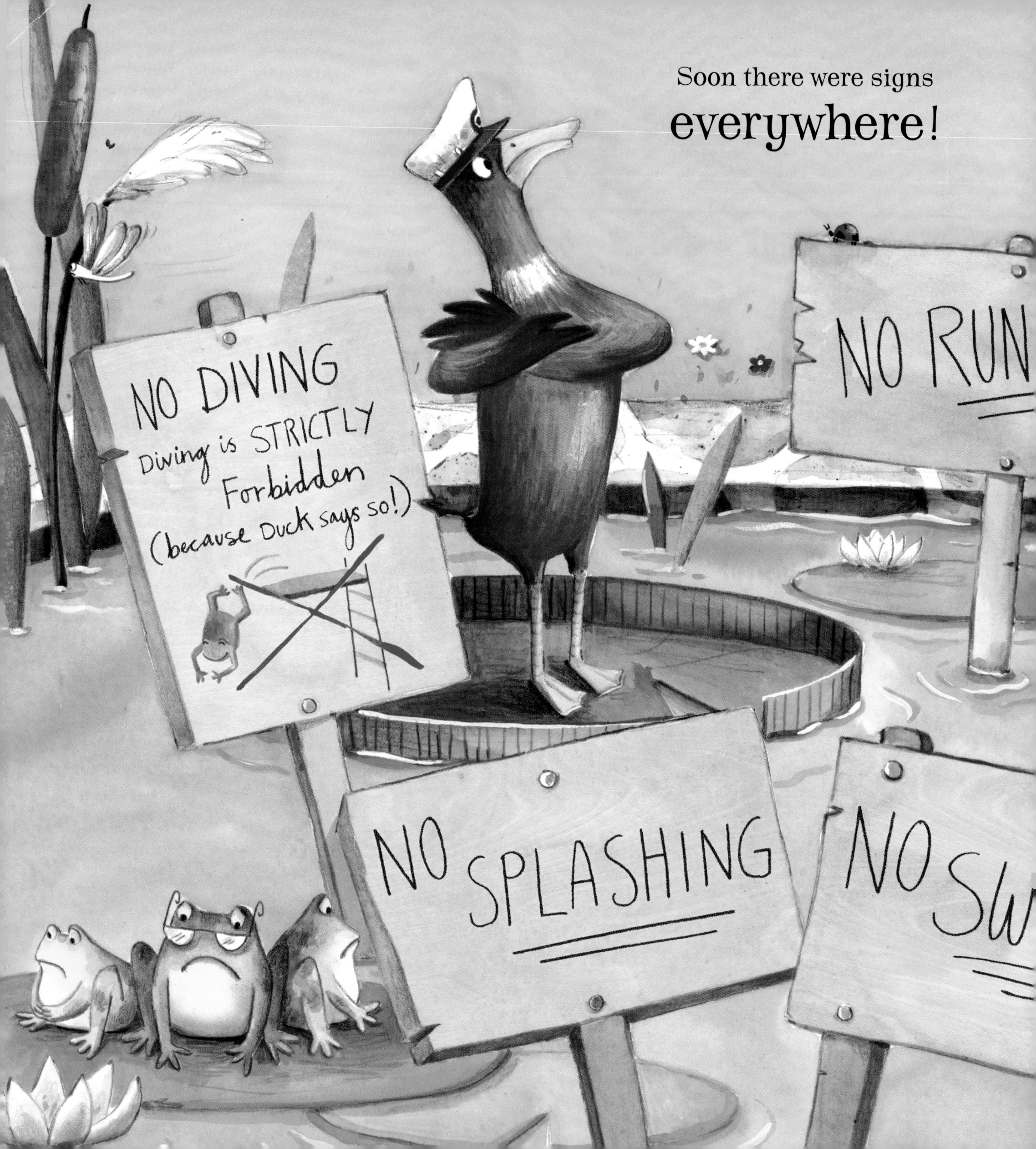

Duck sat down happily.
"Peace at last!" he thought.
There was
not a splash,
buzz, or
plop to be heard.

In fact there was
nothing
to be heard. It was
much
too
quiet!

"Where is everyone?"
wailed Duck. "What have I done?"
He jumped up in a panic and
flew off to find his friends.

NO FISHING
DUCK'S RULE (must be obeyed)

RACING!
der of Duck
(in charge of pond)

As Duck reached the meadow, he saw
them playing together.

"This is fun," buzzed the dragonflies.
"No bossy Duck telling us off!"
croaked the frogs.

A tear fell down Duck's cheek. With a heavy heart he turned around and waddled back to Goose's pond.

The friends were snoozing in the afternoon sun
when they heard hammering coming from the pond.
"Can you believe it?" muttered the frogs.
"Duck is putting up **more** signs!"

The banging went on deep into the night.
Next morning there was an **enormous**
sign in the meadow...

Duck is Very, Very SORRY!

PLEASE COME BACK.

This message is for

the dragonflies,

frogs, and

kingfisher,
from Duck

When the friends arrived at
Goose's pond, they saw
other signs, too:

RACING welcome

FREE fishing rods

NEW diving board

RUNNING,
JUMPING,
SWIMMING, and
SPLASHING
Allowed!

"Silly Duck!"
chirped Kingfisher.
"We've missed you!"
"Even though you were **very** bossy,"
chuckled the frogs.

When Goose came back from vacation,
she said, "Duck, you've done a **grand job**!
I'll leave you in charge next time."

"No, thank you, Goose," Duck laughed. "Being in charge is much too hard!"

And from that day on, Goose's pond was the **happiest** pond in the world, and Duck never said another bossy word. Well, almost never.